A Beginning-to-Read Book

Let's Go, Dear Dragon

by Margaret Hillert

Illustrated by Jack Pullan

NORWOOD HOUSE PRESS

DEAR CAREGIVER,

The books in this Beginning-to-Read collection may look somewhat familiar in that the original versions could have been a part of your own early reading experiences. These carefully written texts feature common sight words to provide your child multiple exposures to the words appearing most frequently in written text. These new versions have been updated and the engaging illustrations are highly appealing to a contemporary audience of young readers.

Begin by reading the story to your child, followed by letting him or her read familiar words and soon your child will be able to read the story independently. At each step of the way, be sure to praise your reader's efforts to build his or her confidence as an independent reader. Discuss the pictures and encourage your child to make connections between the story and his or her own life. At the end of the story, you will find reading activities and a word list that will help your child practice and strengthen beginning reading skills. These activities, along with the comprehension questions are aligned to current standards, so reading efforts at home will directly support the instructional goals in the classroom.

Above all, the most important part of the reading experience is to have fun and enjoy it!

Shannon Cannon

Shannon Cannon,
Literacy Consultant

Norwood House Press • www.norwoodhousepress.com
Beginning-to-Read™ is a registered trademark of Norwood House Press.
Illustration and cover design copyright ©2017 by Norwood House Press. All Rights Reserved.

Authorized adapted reprint from the U.S. English language edition, entitled Let's Go, Dear Dragon by Margaret Hillert. Copyright © 2017 Margaret Hillert. Reprinted with permission. All rights reserved. Pearson and Let's Go, Dear Dragon are trademarks, in the US and/or other countries, of Pearson Education, Inc. or its affiliates. This publication is protected by copyright, and prior permission to re-use in any way in any format is required by both Norwood House Press and Pearson Education. This book is authorized in the United States for use in schools and public libraries.

LIBRARY OF CONGRESS CATALOGING-IN-PUBLICATION DATA

Names: Hillert, Margaret, author. | Pullan, Jack, illustrator.
Title: Let's go, Dear Dragon / by Margaret Hillert ; illustrated by Jack Pullan.
Description: Chicago, IL : Norwood House Press, [2016] | Series: A beginning-to-read book | Summary: "A boy and his pet dragon celebrate the Fourth of July by going to the beach, having a picnic, and watching fireworks. Completely re-illustrated from original edition. Includes reading activities and a word list"-- Provided by publisher.
Identifiers: LCCN 2015046747 | ISBN 9781599537740 (library edition : alk. paper) | ISBN 9781603579001 (ebook)
Subjects: | CYAC: Fourth of July--Fiction. | Dragons--Fiction. | Seashore--Fiction.
Classification: LCC PZ7.H558 Le 2016 | DDC [E]--dc23
LC record available at https://lccn.loc.gov/2015046747

288N—072016
Manufactured in the United States of America in North Mankato, Minnesota.

Get up.
Get up.
This is a big day.
A big day for us.

Here.
Help me with this.
Make it go up.
Up, up, up.

And now come here.
Here is one for you.
You can have this one.

See what Mother and Father can do.
Mother and Father can make something.
Something good.
And we can help.

We work here, too.
Father and I work.
The car looks good.

Get in the car now.
Get in with me.
We will ride, ride, ride.
We will have fun.

Away we go.
Away, away, away.
What a good day.

Here we are.
We can play here.

Look what I can do to you.
No one can see you now.
No one can guess where you are.

See this.
I can make it go.
It can go up and up.
Get it.
Get it.

Oh, my.
Look what you can do.
You are good at this.

We can do this, too.
Work, work, work.
We can do it.

Oh, oh, oh.
Help, help.
Look at us now.
That dragon is too good.

Come with me now.
Come in here.
You will like it.

Go, go, go.
Help me go.
I like to do this.

This looks good.
I want this—
and this—
and this.

You are a big help.
A big, big help.
Now you have one, too.
It is fun to eat.

Oh, look at that!
Do you see that?
Can you do that?
Yes, you can.
You can do it, too.

One, two, three.
GO!
No, that is not good.
That is too little.

Now, here we go.
One, two, three.
Oh, my!
Oh, my!
Look at that!
That is good!

Here you are with me.
And here I am with you.
Oh, what a happy day, Dear Dragon.

The following activities support the findings of the National Reading Panel that determined the most effective components for reading instruction are: Phonemic Awareness, Phonics, Vocabulary, Fluency, and Text Comprehension.

Phonemic Awareness: The /g/ sound

Oral Blending: Say the beginning and ending sounds of the following words and ask your child to listen to the sounds and say the whole word:

ba + /g/ = bag	di + /g/ = dig	sa + /g/ = sag
bi + /g/ = big	le + /g/ = leg	ta + /g/ = tag
pe + /g/ = peg	dra + /g/ = drag	fla + /g/ = flag

Phonics: The letter Gg

1. Demonstrate how to form the letters **G** and **g** for your child.

2. Have your child practice writing **G** and **g** at least three times each.

3. Ask your child to point to the words in the book that start with the letter **g**.

4. Write down the following words and ask your child to circle the letter **g** in each word:

go	glad	tag	get	flag	guess
tiger	give	target	gave	dig	got
rag	gum	finger	good		

Vocabulary: Homophones

1. Find the words *to, too,* and *two* in the book. Read the sentences that include each word.

2. Explain to your child that words that sound the same but have different meanings are called homophones.

3. Write each word on a piece of paper. Say sentences including each word and ask your child to point to the correct word for each sentence. For example, which one goes with "I am going (to) the store." Or "There are (two) shoes in a pair."

Fluency: Choral Reading

1. Reread the story with your child at least two more times while your child tracks the print by running a finger under the words as they are read. Ask your child to read the words he or she knows with you.

2. Reread the story aloud together. Be careful to read at a rate that your child can keep up with.

3. Repeat choral reading and allow your child to be the lead reader and ask him or her to change from a whisper to a loud voice while you follow along and change your voice.

Text Comprehension: Discussion Time

1. Ask your child to retell the sequence of events in the story.

2. To check comprehension, ask your child the following questions:

   • What is the object that the boy and Dear Dragon made go up the pole?

   • What holiday do you think the family is celebrating? What happened in the story to make you think that?

   • How did Dear Dragon help on page 23?

   • What is your favorite holiday? Why?

WORD LIST

***Let's Go, Dear Dragon* uses the 64 words listed below.**

This list can be used to practice reading the words that appear in the text. You may wish to write the words on index cards and use them to help your child build automatic word recognition. Regular practice with these words will enhance your child's fluency in reading connected text.

a	eat	I	oh	up
am		in	one	us
and	Father	is		
are	for	it	play	want
at	fun			we
away		like	ride	what
	get	little		where
big	go	look(s)	see	will
	good		something	with
can	guess	make		work
car		me	that	
come	happy	Mother	the	yes
	have	my	this	you
day	help		three	
dear	here	no	to	
do		not	too	
dragon		now	two	

ABOUT THE AUTHOR Margaret Hillert has helped millions of children all over the world learn to read independently. She was a first grade teacher for 34 years and during that time started writing books that her students could both gain confidence in reading and enjoy. She wrote well over 100 books for children just learning to read. As a child, she enjoyed writing poetry and continued her poetic writings as an adult for both children and adults.

Photograph by Glenna Washburn

ABOUT THE ILLUSTRATOR A talented and creative illustrator, Jack Pullan, is a graduate of William Jewell College. He has also studied informally at Oxford University and the Kansas City Art Institute. He was mentored by the renowned watercolor artists, Jim Hamil and Bill Amend. Jack's work has graced the pages of many enjoyable children's books, various educational materials, cartoon strips, as well as many greeting cards. Jack currently resides in Kansas.